Ex Libris

Lenore A. McGown

People I'd Like to Keep

MARY O'NEILL

People I'd Like to Keep

ILLUSTRATED BY PAUL GALDONE

Doubleday & Company Inc.   Garden City, New York

Library of Congress Catalog Card Number 63–12991   Copyright © 1964 by
Mary O'Neill   Illustrations Copyright © 1964 by Paul Galdone
All Rights Reserved   Printed in the United States of America   First Edition

Besides friends and mothers and fathers, sisters and
brothers, there are some others I want to keep.
So, before I grow up and get crowded, I think the
best way is to write them all down today . . .

The Balloon Man

Mister balloon man
Isn't his name
But it's close to it
As I ever came.
On Saturday morning
Rain or shine
He sits on a corner
Right near mine
In purple sweater
And checkered cap
With a thousand balloons
In his fat-legged lap
And up from his fingers
Laced with strings
Globes of color
Without wings
Bump the rooftops
Nudge the sky—
Impatiently
We wait to buy.

"One for a nickel
Three for a dime
Looka! Looka!
Dem tings climb!"
No nickel for candy
No nickel for cone
One nickel a week
And one nickel alone—
But as long as he sits
On the corner near mine
On Saturday morning
Rain or shine
I'll have a balloon
A big red one to fly
Over the rooftops
Into the sky. . . .

Darling Doctor
de Plunkett

When my brother Joey broke his arm
And walked around with a sling
He suddenly became a much
TOO IMPORTANT thing!
My mother helped him with his clothes,
My father cut his meat
And everyone who came to call
Brought *him* a treat.
And it was just as bad as this
At school and out on the street—
Everyone looking at Joey and saying:
"How brave! . . . How sweet!"
But no one noticed my kneecap
Swollen and black and blue
Or remembered I'd climbed the same tree
And fallen out of it, too.
No one in the whole world
Cared what happened to *me*
(Without a sling one simply can't
Suffer *importantly*).

I held myself bent over
And learned to limp with grace
And I let a little misery
Clutter up my face.
But did my mother notice?
No! No! No! No! No!
She had eyes for only
That sling-on-the-arm-of-a-Joe!
And did my father wonder
Why I was listless and sad?
He didn't. Yet I'm the only
Daughter he ever had!
"The pain will go away, Joey,
In just a day or two.
Pretty soon, my brave boy,
You'll be as good as new!"
When I showed my kneecap:
"That's a nasty bruise you've got,"
Both of them idly muttered
And then they just forgot.

But Doctor de Plunkett knows suffering
Where it *doesn't* show
Because he said to my mother:
"Mrs. B. do you know
Susie's sprung her heartstrings
And I should put on a sling,
But her injury's so deep down
I cannot reach the thing!
There's no prescription for it
Except a rocking chair
Mixed with the blue of twilight
And the two of you
Sitting there. . . ."

Paddy,
the Railroad-Crossing Watchman

One winter evening
(Snow-dark at four)
I was walking home
From the grocery store
And a train cried out
As they always do:
"WHO . . . WHOO . . . WHOOO
ARE . . . YOU . . . OOO?"

It was free
And fast and wild
I was hidden
In a child
Wanting to laugh
Longing to cry
Having to see
That train go by
Waltzing and spitting
Soot and spark
Into the tangly
Winter dark . . .
And I didn't know
Or forgot to care
How fast my feet
Had carried me there
When Paddy, the watchman,
Pulled all of me back
As the gates went down
On the railroad track
And onions shocked
From the grocery sack . . .
A lantern swung
And a panther cried
I wanted to look
And I wanted to hide
And I felt Paddy
At my side
His frozen glove
Against my mitt
Had some of the strength
Of God in it. . . .

In roars of iron
And swirls of smoke
The beautiful-terrible
Engine spoke
Whirling down
The marabou track
Flinging snow and
Cinders back
Pulling cars
So live with light
They wound a sash
Around the night
And in each one
Against the glass
I saw the lovely
Travelers pass:

Oh bright and
Fascinating blur
Of men and women
Silks and fur
Feasting silver
Snowy beds
With little lights
Above their heads.
The dining rooms
Where people ate
Had curls of parsley
On each plate—
I saw hats and
Pocketbooks,
Conductors, passengers
And cooks,
Some rubbed golden
Panes to see
Darkness, lantern,
Watchman, me.

"Do you think," I said
As the last train light
Winked its ruby
Out of sight,
"I'll ever be on
A train at night?
That engine, whistle,
Flying spark
Will pull me through
The darling dark
To a place I see
Behind my eyes
That is all wonder
And surprise?"

"Ye'll traipse off on
A Diesel train
Twice as grand as
This again.
Ye'll be bonnier
By far
Than any of
Yon travelers are.
Flyin' airplanes
Will be proud
To hold ye up
Against a cloud. . . .
There'll be blinker lights
At crossin's then
And no more need
For watcher men!

Now pocket the onions
And coddle the bread
Ye've a long, long
Journey up ahead
An' time is flyin' . . ."
Paddy said
Swinging his lantern
And making a glow
Of wild summer roses
On top of the snow.

The Circus People

After the afternoon circus
In the first beginning of night
We short-cutted home through our pasture
And saw a wonderful sight:

The girl that swung from the high trapeze
Up to the scary heights
Sat on the steps of a caravan
Mending her spangled tights.

As the Bird Man petted
His cockatoo
His black crows squawked:
"Me too! . . . Me too!"

A Dwarf sat on
The Fat Lady's lap
Knitting himself a
Stocking cap.

The Strong Man hung
A shirt to dry,
And the Tallest-Man-in-the-World
Walked by.

Across the tents
Tree lights were strung
The circus supper
Had begun.
Acrobats and clowns
And kings
Were eating ordinary
Things:
Hamburgers and
Lima beans,
Buttered buns and
Turnip greens.

Off in the shadows
Behind bars
The eyes of leopards
Stared like stars,
And when the keepers
Rattled pails
All the lions
Thumped their tails!

Something touched me
On the sleeve
In this world of
Make-believe
And I jumped,
Looked up to see
An elephant was
Nudging me!

A circus cook
In a floury cap
Gave my brother and me
A gingersnap.

The manager cried:
"Be off! Away!
A circus lot's no
Place to play!"
The Human Fly said:
"Let them be!
Didn't you never
Want to see
What's behind
The scenery?"

We saw lady giraffes
With lockets,
And kangaroos with
Empty pockets
Learning to waltz
Around a ring—and
That was about the
Funniest thing!

A Gladiator
Watched himself
From a mirror
On a shelf
And tried on several
Smiles to see
Which one fit most
Handsomely!

Then we heard Father's
Cows commence
A mooing racket
Near the fence,
And saw the zebras
Black and white
Meadow-munching
In the night.
For this the cows
Were not prepared—
They just clumped and mooed
And stared.

My brother braver
Than a bear
Coaxed the zebras
Back to where
The Circus People
Waved a light.
They were so grateful
And polite
Shouting: "Thank you!"
And, "Good-by!
Both be good
And have a care
We'll all meet again
Somewhere. . . ."

Uggle

Uggle is a blanket
Worn to shreds
It's been on every
One of my beds.
Once it went off
In a Good Will pack
And I had an awful time
Getting it back.
Once it was tossed
In an old trash bin
But I saw its fringe
And climbed right in.
Once it was bitten
By a moth
And once it was used
As a dusting cloth!
Why did I love it
More than my cat,
My dog, my doll and my
Sunday hat?
Because when dark
Night shadows flung
Monsters on walls
When I was young
It was to Uggle
That I clung. . . .

Later when I
Was four or five
And *knew* that
Shadows weren't alive
Uggle was part
Of every night
Like the stars and
The bedside light,
Like loving eyes and
A hand held tight. . . .
Like somebody, almost,
But not quite. . . .

The Milk Man's Little Boy

I just love our milk-bill days
Then I see the boy who talks *two ways*.
He and his father come up the walk
Doing their family finger talk,
The boy rings the bell, says: "How do you do?
We've come to collect milk money from you."
When my mother says: "Now, what do we owe?"
You should see the way his fingers go—
Like acrobats and elastic bands
As he asks his father with his hands!
His father answers with fingers flying
And in an instant the boy's replying.

My mother pays from her open purse
And remarks the heat is getting worse.
His father wipes the sweat from his face
Then with lightning speed and dazzling grace
His fingers do a jig of joy
Before the eyes of his little boy
And the little boy turns to us to say:
"My father says: 'Thank you and good day!'"

The Hurdy-Gurdy Man

The street's small-town New England
The names on letter plates
Read: Holloway and Hathaway,
Sheffield, Jones and Gates.
The houses are all high and white
The people tall and spare,
And even on a summer day
There's coolness in the air.
He wears a scarlet sweater
And black, crisp, clock-spring hair,
His eyes are brown and brazen,
And half his arms are bare!
His cheeks are red as roses,
His teeth a flashing white—
His skin an olive, *glacé* glove
Fits new and smooth and tight.

His walk is almost swagger,
He brings a precious thing,
Strange and bright and beautiful
To each New England Spring!
A monkey on his shoulder,
An organ strapped in place
Set with pearl and mica and
A foreign woman's face!
O Barcarole! O Sole Mio!
O Barber of Seville!
The world beyond the one we know
Beneath our window sill!
He comes without a warning
Any time in May
Cranks his hurdy-gurdy
To make the music play—
The monkey on his shoulder
Rattles his tin cup
Then hops along the sidewalk
To pick the pennies up.

The ladies in the houses
On the elm-sun-speckled street
Stand behind lace curtains
Shadowy, discreet . . .
Then fling aside their dusters
And keep time with their feet!
Children rush the doorways
Some even dare the walk
But none will ever touch him
And none will ever talk—
But our pennies speak
In a lovely rain
Calling and calling him
Back again. . . .

Miss Hortense Rogers,

the Grade School Principal

"Why did you do it?"
The principal said
And I beside her
Sick with dread
Stared at the hair
On top of her head
A tumble-down mountain
Part gray, part red.
"Strange actions for
A little lass
The best behaved of
All her class!

Why did you pinch
Little Johnny Carew?
He's never been known
To bother you.
And you stuck out your tongue
At your teacher, too.
Why did you grab
Emmy Rimini's ball,
And trip her coming
Down the hall?"
On her wall George Washington's bust
Was covered with sunshine and with dust.
On her desk a cut-glass vase
Held the chopped-up parts of the principal's face.
"Is it because young
Johnny Carew
Doesn't walk home from school
With you?
It couldn't be *that*—
Or could it be?
How old was I when
That happened to me?"
I think she was thumbing
Through her mind
For something lost that
She had to find,
Because for a while
She stood real still
With her hands on the edge
Of the window sill

And when she turned
I could sort of see
The third-grade girl
She used to be,
With bright red hair
And hoppity feet
Running down a
Village street
Smelling things that
Teased her nose
In the time of the
Butterfly
And the rose. . . .

Running and running
Through a wood
Back to the place where
Both of us stood,
In the principal's room
On the second floor
Where her name in gold
Is on the door.
"Envy's a horrible weed,"
She said.
"With a snaky stem and a
Monster's head—
Dig it out and
Throw it away.
Tell them you're sorry and
Mean what you say."

Swollen with tears
I could not speak
And then she kissed me
On the cheek!
Miss Hortense Rogers,
Miss Principal Thing
Friend of my first
Lovelorn spring.

Mrs. Brown

Mrs. Brown is a lady
Freckled and fat
With too many flowers
On too big of a hat.
She wears cinnamon skirts
And bright-stone rings
And a wonderful lot of
Hand-down things.
She lives in the broken
Part of town
Where Poverty's tearing
The houses down—
But she wouldn't live
Any other place
And happiness blooms
All over her face.
She comes to our house
One day a week
To iron and scrub
And kiss my cheek
And she always brings me
A thing or two
She's polished so
It looks like new:
A paper rose or an
Oyster shell,
A shiny button,
A jingle bell;

And she always has
A story to tell
About her brother
Who went to sea,
And the accident that
Limped her knee
And how her little dog
Cried and cried
The terrible night
Her husband died;
And how a man
By the name of Jim
Presumed she'd marry
The likes of him.

She talks about people
Until I see
Them moving around
Inside of me,
On the merry-go-round
Of memory:
The beggars, the widows,
The pawnshop, the bums,
The sweetness of Christmas
When it comes. . . .
And when she's scrubbed and
Ironed our clothes
She washes her hands
And blows her nose
And I show her the chip
In the rosebud cup
And she says of course
She can use it up,
So she tucks it among
The hand-down things
In a shopping bag
She always brings

Then she counts her hours
With a pencil stub
That hangs by a string
At the laundry tub—
Collects her money,
Winks her eye
Claps on her hat
And says good-by
And I wish someone
Could tell me why
Whenever she leaves
I always cry. . . ?

... *there's the*

Woman with The Walk

The woman with The Walk
Sells pencils in the park
And she never leaves her bench
Until after dark.
All day she sits
With a shawl on her lap
And when she isn't busy
She takes a little nap.
She keeps her money
In a bent tin cup
And when you go by
She holds pencils up.
She says: "Fine pencils,
Red, green, blue,
Each one of them longing
To write for You!"

She carries her lunch
In a newspaper pack
And a cushion to soften
The iron at her back,
And a black umbrella
That's also a cane,
A shade for the sun and
A roof for the rain.
When I'm with other people
I walk the other way
Because she always asks me
How I am today.
But when I'm alone
With a nickel to spare
And you're looking for me
You'll find me there.
That's how I found out
Why she lingers on
When all her customers
Are gone;

Why she waits for the
Empty, supper-time street—
It's because she has
Two unmatched feet!
One's like a weight
That holds her down,
Big and lumpy and
Booted in brown—
This one she hides
In her droopy shawl,
But her other foot isn't
Crippled at all!
And when the day is
Almost done
She lets her pretty foot
Have some fun!
Safe in the dark from
Passing glances
You should see how
That foot dances
All by itself and
Shapes an arc
And a little star in the
Dust in the park.
Then she stands and
Her long skirts fall
Until you can't see
Her feet at all—

And the good foot
Like a diving swallow
Leads with a step
The boot can't follow!
And I can almost
Hear her say:
"Behave good foot
You've had your play. . . ."
As she limps off in
Her up-and-down way. . . .

My Friend, Leona

Leona knows the alleys
Where people eat and sleep
In helter-skelter houses
And the company they keep.
She knows a hump-back beggar
And a Welfare man,
A lady who tells fortunes
With a peacock-feather fan
And she can raise geraniums
In a tomato can.
She says she has ribbons
Wide as my hand
But she fastens her hair
With a rubber band.
She says she has dresses
Too sweet to be seen
But the ones she wears
Are scrimped and mean.
She says her home
Is huge and fair
But at present she's
Not living there.

She says it's beautiful
Grand and neat
With seven white pillars
Set back from the street,
With willow trees arching
The elegant drive
Silvering people
As they arrive . . .
That her father's the captain
Of a ship
Off on a long
Mysterious trip . . .
That her mother's a princess
In disguise
Making and peddling
Blueberry pies.

Her mother has beaten
Her black and blue
For saying things
That are not true
But Leona shouts back:
"Yes, they are, too!
I can see them plainer
Than day-old bread
Or the plaster peeling
Over my head!"
And then Leona
Will snuffle and try
To explain that she can't
Always rely
On what comes to her
By ear or by eye.

Then her mother says:
"You'll have no more to do
With the saying of things
That are not true.
You know what happens
To people like you?
Shunned and set in the midst
Of strife—
Is that what you
Want out of life?"
Leona's head
Which she holds so high
Droops as these words
Go stabbing by.
Her shoulders sag
And the big surprise
That lights Leona
Goes out of her eyes.

And I am afraid
Some awful day
My friend, Leona,
Will stay that way.
Leona's a liar
Some people say
But I think of her
Another way:
Just ask Leona the
Way to a place—
There'll be no lie
In the map she'll trace.
When lessons are far
Too hard to do
Leona's answers come
Out true.
And when the truth
Stings like a bee
She'd never tell it on
You or me.
Leona makes over
Things she can't bear
All ugly streets
And ratted hair
All frightened things
And things that glare
The hole in the carpet
And the chair.
All broken ones
Who sit and stare
From window sills in
Their underwear.

Listen to her
And you'll see
Everything as it
Wants to be . . .
Leona's tall and her eyes are blue
And if you knew Leona you'd love her, too!

Miss Norma Jean Pugh,

First Grade Teacher

Full of oatmeal
And gluggy with milk
On a morning in springtime
Soft as silk
When legs feel slow
And bumble bees buzz
And your nose tickles from
Dandelion fuzz
And you long to
Break a few
Cobwebs stuck with
Diamond dew
Stretched right out
In front of you—
When all you want
To do is *feel*
Until it's time for
Another meal,
Or sit right down
In the cool
Green grass
And watch the
Caterpillars pass. . . .

Who cares if
Two and two
Are four or five
Or red or blue?
Who cares whether
Six or seven
Come before or after
Ten or eleven?
Who cares if
C-A-T
Spells cat or rat
Or tit or tat
Or ball or bat?
Well, I do
But I didn't
Used to—
Until MISS NORMA JEAN PUGH!
She's terribly old
As people go
Twenty-one-or-five-or-six
Or so
But she makes a person want to
KNOW!

Mr. Zinnia

Mr. Zinnia lives somewhere
As everyone does
But each day his address is
Not where it was.
His home is wherever
He is when it's dark:
A boxcar, a warehouse,
A bench in the park,
The arch of a bridge
Or wherever there's space
To hold a man resting
Securely in place.
He has sea-color eyes
And a long pointy nose
The rest of him's lost
In other men's clothes
Wound and pinned-over and
Tied up with string—
And he comes out of hiding
Like bears, in the spring.

"Madame," he says when
We answer the door,
"I'm back to wash windows and
Polish the floor,
Furbish the cellar,
Scour down the crocks,
Sweep off the sidewalk
And tune up the clocks.

I hope, lovely ladies,
Good fortune has cast
Golden rings round you
Since I saw you last!"
"It has," says my mother
"But I have a hunch
In your hurry to get here
You went without lunch.
Here, let me give you
A nice plate of stew
Hunger makes work
So much harder to do."
"How thoughtful, my lady,
How thoughtful, indeed,
And I from my travels
Have fetched you some seed."
He dives in his pocket
He brings out his hand
Full of brown flutters and
Lint balls and sand.
"Zinnias!" he says
As some people say, "Gold!"

"There was never a posy
As tough or as bold
As giving of color
As sparse in its needs
As one with the earth
As these little seeds!
So, plant 'em, my lady,
Pretend when they float
Their color on summer
You're reading a note
Scribbled in flowers that
A wanderer wrote
Stamped with the sunshine
Sealed with the dew
And deep into autumn
Still thanking you!"

Mr. Zinnia ate faster
Than I ever do
In less than a minute
He'd vanished the stew
Mopped up the gravy
With bittens of bread
Wiped off his fingers
And leaned back his head,
And sleepily, whispery,
Dreamy he said:
"I saw me a desert,
I saw me a bird
With the sweetest song
I ever heard
I saw me a salmon
Leap ten feet
In wrinkled-up water
Wild and sweet
I saw where the sea
And a mountain meet
And the sea like a girl
Cat-curling, neat
With shimmering hair
And young sharp teeth
Tossing a shell and
A seaweed wreath
On the dark wet sand
At the mountain's feet—

Some nights are cold
And some are long
But there's always this little
Tra-la-la song
Under the snowflake
Over the dawn
And it rushes me, pushes me
On and on. . . ."
He scrubs the floor
He mows the lawn and
Before we're used to him
He's gone. . . .

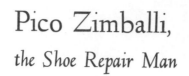

Pico Zimballi,

the Shoe Repair Man

You walk down the street
And stop at the door
Lettered: Z I M B A L L I —
And that's Pico's store.
It smells of old leather
New leather and shoe
Garlic and polish and
Rubber and glue.
It's dusty and crowded
The sofa is split
And so piled with repairings
There's no place to sit.
Filmy Rome, linty Naples
Hang on the wall
Tilted, bedraggled and
Ready to fall
Between them a sandal
Ripped at the toe
Swings by a cross strap
Now to, and now fro.

The shelves are covered
The counter is too
With the wrinkles and wearings
That walking will do—
And sitting among them
Bent almost in two
Is Pico Zimballi
Re-soling a shoe.
He looks up and smiles and
Says: "How do you do?"
And "What, little one, can
Pico do for you?"
I can't say: "Just let me
See you punching holes
With an awl through the leather
Of somebody's soles!"
I can't say: "Please let me
See shiny nails slip
One by one as you need them
From over your lip!"

Or: "Could I hold your hammer
And give it a pound
That rattles the room with
A thump-thumpy sound?"
I can't say: "Does cowhide
Falling in scrap
Remind you of jig-sawed
Parts of a map?"
Or: "Pico Zimballi
Where is your home?
Did you once live in Naples?
Or once live in Rome?"
Or: "Are you a gypsy?
Is it really true
That the print of a person
Is stamped in his shoe?"
He isn't unfriendly
But somehow I know
He finished his happiness
Long time ago.
Beyond his politeness
He slams a small door
And nothing but shoes ever
Clutter his store.
So I say: "Shoelaces"
"Half soles" or "Hello!"
Wait for them, pay for them,
Take them and go.

Wishing and wishing
He'd sort of unbend
And tell me because I'm a
Beginning friend
Why it was
He had to flee
From a castle
Cross the sea. . . .
Was he once
A gypsy king?
Or an even more
Important thing?
Did an empire
Fall apart
Because he had a
Broken heart?

You walk down the street
And stop at the door
Lettered: Z I M B A L L I
And that's Pico's store—
There a silvery bell will
Tinkle you in,
And I hope the soles
Of your shoes are thin
Then you'll have time
To think and stare,
And afterward I'll
Meet you there.
We'll smile at each other
And off we'll go
And then you'll tell me
What I already know:
That anyone with a
Good pair of eyes
Knows Pico Zimballi's a
Prince in disguise. . . .

Mister Adolph Brunner,

the Bakery Man

Mister Brunner is a baker
He lives in Evertown
Where all the buns have icing
And all bread crusts are brown.
Mister Brunner smells of nutmeg
Of cinnamon and clove,
Raisins, yeast and walnuts and
The warmness of a stove.
All his clerking ladies
Cash-register each sale,
And slice off little portions
That overtip the scale.
Twelve's a proper dozen
The weight's exactly right,
Like imitation nurses
In cold and starchy white
They rustle off together
At five o'clock at night.

Nut
Lay

Then Mrs. Brunner enters
And climbs upon a stool.
In the bakery back room
The ovens start to cool.
She becomes the wrapper
Mister Brunner takes the trade
And that's when all his lifelong
Customers are made!
Then thirteen is a dozen
And a currant bun's for free—
If you're very skinny
You'll probably get *three*!
Once a giant puff paste
Skimmed with sugar lace
Crouched upon a doily
In Mister Brunner's case.

Staring I imagined every
Crispy-creamy bite
I had just the price of bread
In my fist that night.
"Please a loaf of seeded rye,
The crustiest you've got."
He gave it to me then he said:
"Here's something you forgot!"
I looked. The giant puff paste
Skimmed with sugar lace
Was no longer on its doily
In Mister Brunner's case!
I went home the long way
On lazy, poky feet
Licking off the sugar
That floated choky, sweet
Above the crackling pastry
Of this enormous treat,
Delaying, longing, itching
To crunch it with my teeth—
(Oh! delicious moment
When cream-and-crispy meet.
And nobody's counting
The bites that you eat!)

I sauntered home
Put down the bread
With selfish whirlings
In my head.
I looked at little brothers
And little sisters, too
At first I felt quite horrid
Then suddenly I knew
That knowing Mister Brunner
As very well I do
They'd had the same experience
I'd just been through!